Early Reader titles are ideal for childre[n]
existing phonics knowledge to practise
sentences with help. Each book uses a
repeated and decodable words to steadily build reading confidence.

Special features:

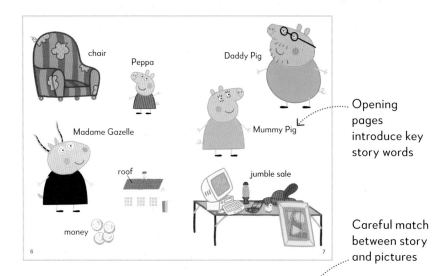

Opening pages introduce key story words

Careful match between story and pictures

"Can we take this old chair, too, Daddy?" says Peppa.

"No! This is a very good chair," says Daddy Pig.

Large, clear type

Ladybird

Educational Consultants: Geraldine Taylor and James Clements
Book Banding Consultant: Kate Ruttle

LADYBIRD BOOKS
UK | USA | Canada | Ireland | Australia
India | New Zealand | South Africa

Ladybird Books is part of the Penguin Random House group of companies
whose addresses can be found at global.penguinrandomhouse.com.

www.penguin.co.uk   www.puffin.co.uk   www.ladybird.co.uk

Text adapted from *Peppa Pig: Daddy Pig's Old Chair* first published by Ladybird Books Ltd 2008
Read It Yourself edition first published by Ladybird Books Ltd 2014
This edition published 2024
001

Printed in China

The authorized representative in the EEA is Penguin Random House Ireland,
Morrison Chambers, 32 Nassau Street, Dublin D02 YH68

A CIP catalogue record for this book is available from the British Library

ISBN: 978-0-241-56535-3

All correspondence to:
Ladybird Books
Penguin Random House Children's
One Embassy Gardens, 8 Viaduct Gardens, London SW11 7BW

Daddy Pig's Old Chair

Adapted by Ellen Philpott

 chair

Peppa

Madame Gazelle

roof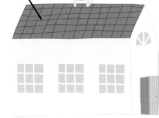

money

6

Daddy Pig

Mummy Pig

jumble sale

"Oh no! We have to get
a new roof for the school,"
says Madame Gazelle.
"We will have a jumble sale
to make money."

9

"My old toys can go to the jumble sale, to make money," says Peppa.

"Can we take this old chair, too, Daddy?" says Peppa.

"No! This is a very good chair," says Daddy Pig.

13

Madame Gazelle takes the old toys for the jumble sale.

"Take this old chair, too," says Mummy Pig.

15

Next, Peppa, Mummy Pig and
Daddy Pig go to the jumble sale.

Peppa's friends go, too.

Daddy Pig's chair is
at the jumble sale.

It looks very old.

19

Peppa and her friends look at the toys.

"Oh! My old toy looks good," says Peppa.

"I will have my old toy,"
says Peppa.

"We will too!" say her friends.

"I will get this new chair," says Daddy. "It will look good next to my old one."

"No. It IS the old one!"
says Mummy Pig.

"Oh no," says Daddy Pig.
"It was so much money!"

"Good," says Madame Gazelle.
"We have so much money.
We can get a new school roof!"

29

How much do you remember about the story of *Peppa Pig: Daddy Pig's Old Chair*? Answer these questions and find out!

- Why is Madame Gazelle having a jumble sale?

- What does Peppa give to the jumble sale?

- What does Daddy Pig buy at the jumble sale?